We can't see the wind,
we hear what it brings.
We can't hear the wind,
we see what it brings.

Other books by anne herbauts
published by Enchanted Lion Books:

Prince Silencio
Monday

What Color Is The Wind?

aиие herbauts • • •

Translated from the French by Claudia Zoe Bedrick

ENCHANTED LION BOOKS

NEW YORK

The little giant sets out early
to search for the wind and its color.

He meets an old dog and asks,
What color is the wind?

It has a color, says the dog.
It is pink, flowery, pale white.

No, says the wolf,
the wind is the dark smell of the forest.

The little giant bumps into an elephant.
He asks, *What color is the wind?*

It is round, cold, gray and smooth, like a pebble.

No, sighs the mountain. It is blue.

The little giant passes through town.
What color is the wind?

The color of curtains, laundry, clothes...

But the window disagrees.
It is the color of time.

So the little giant asks the rain,
What color is the wind?

The rain knows nothing.

But the bees are buzzing:
the wind is the color of sunshine.

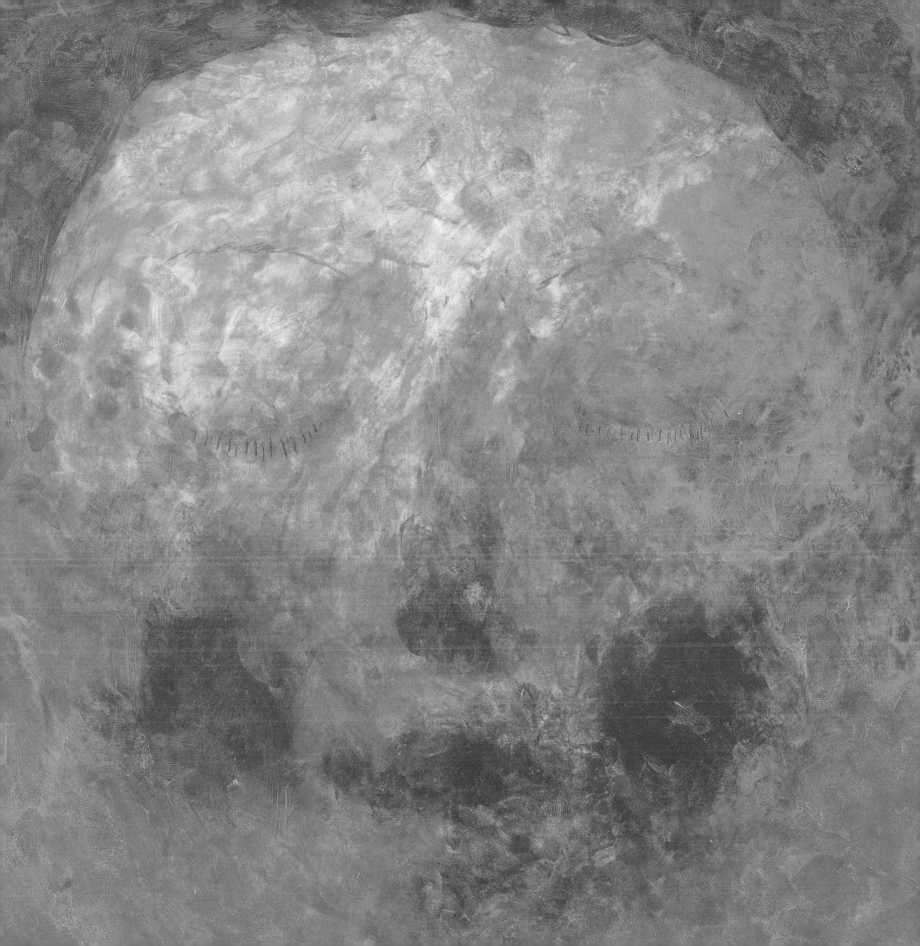

A stream runs by.
What color is the wind?

That of the sky reflected in water.

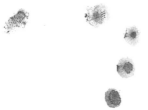

water

water

water

water

The little giant rests at the foot of a tree.
What color is the wind? he sighs.

A sugary color, murmurs the apple tree.

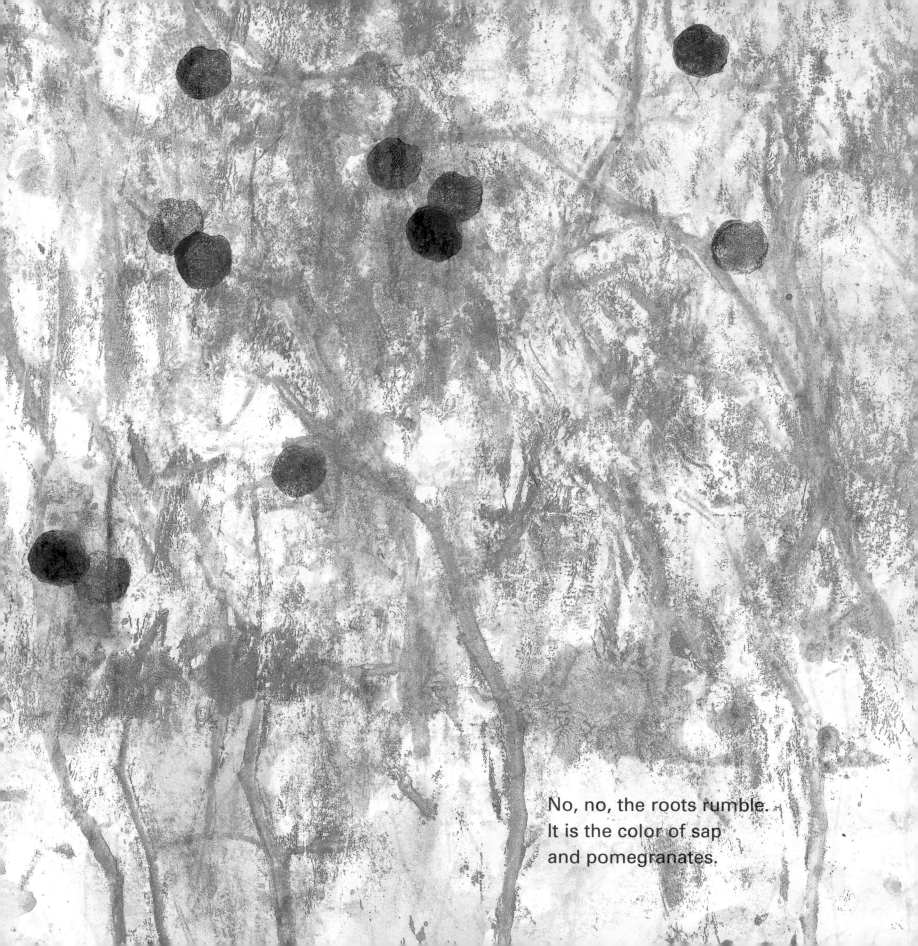

No, no, the roots rumble.
It is the color of sap
and pomegranates.

Then it's gone.

The little giant asks a bird,
What color...

But the bird has flown away.

The little giant comes upon someone
he senses is enormous.
What color is the wind?

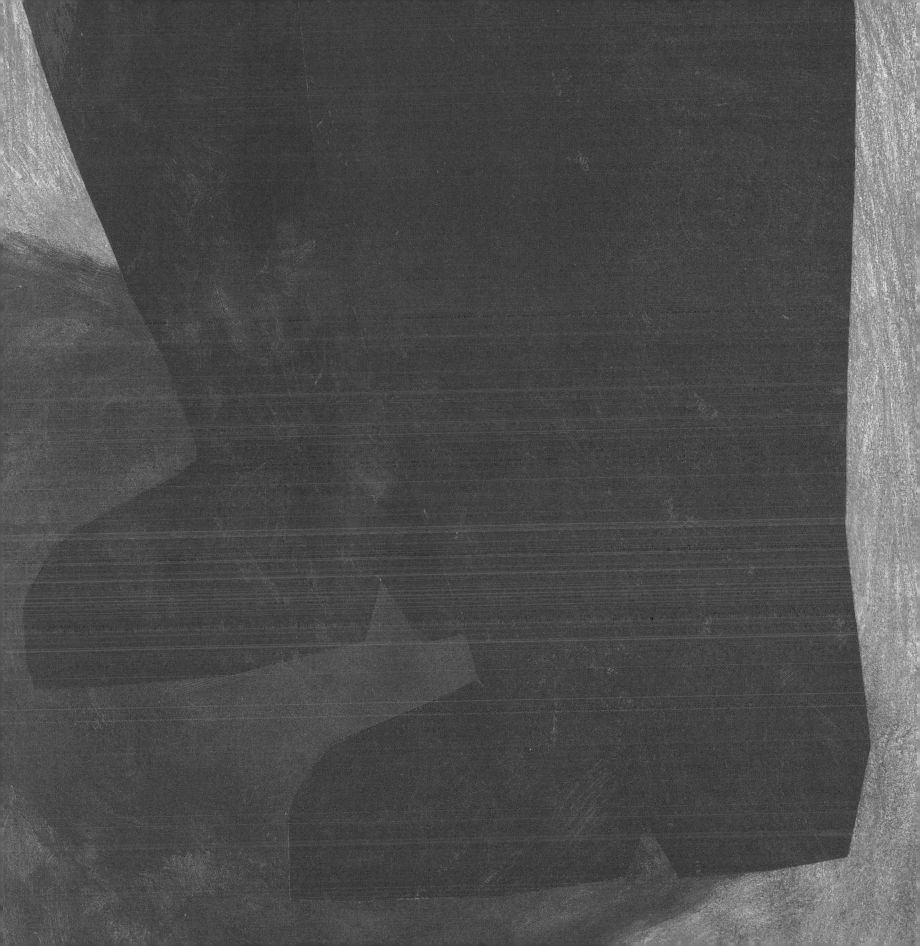

And the enormous giant,
with a slow gesture says:
The color of the wind?

It is everything at once.
This whole book.

Then he takes the book and,
thumb against its edge,
he lets the pages fly.

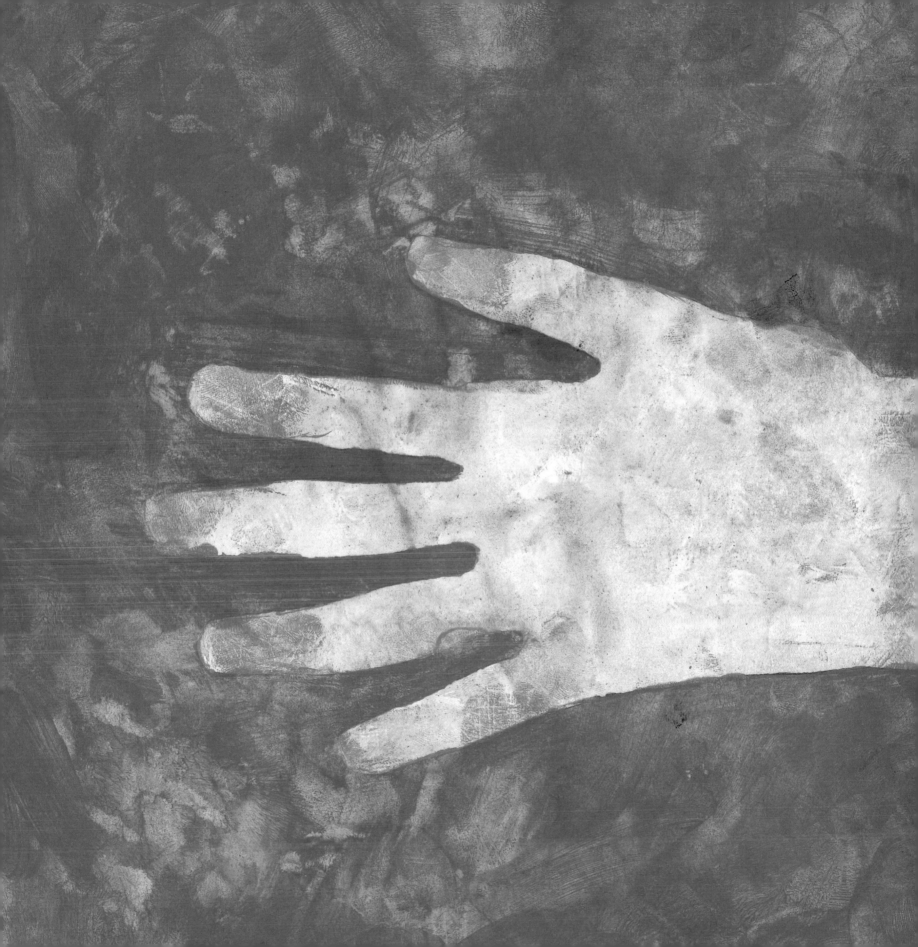

The little giant feels the wind
and its gentleness.

The wind of the book.

Design: Anne Quévy
Layout: Neil Desmet

● ● ●

www.enchantedlion.com

● ● ●

First English-language edition published in 2016 by Enchanted Lion Books,
351 Van Brunt Street, Brooklyn, NY 11231
Copyright © 2016 by Claudia Bedrick for the English-language Translation
Copyright © 2011 by Casterman
Originally published in France in 2011 as de quelle couleur est le vent?
All rights reserved under International and Pan-American Copyright Conventions.
A CIP record is on file with the Library of Congress. ISBN 978-1-59270-221-3

Printed in China by Leo Paper

1 3 5 7 9 10 8 6 4 2

L.10EIFN001958.N001